FRIDAY THE 13TH
FROM THE
BLACK LAGOON®

Get more monster-sized laughs from

The Black Lagoon®

FRIDAY THE 13ᵀᴴ
FROM THE
BLACK LAGOON®

by Mike Thaler
Illustrated by Jared Lee

SCHOLASTIC INC.

For Samantha,
welcome to the world—M.T.

To Dick and Elly Wilson—J.L.

FOX
← WHO
LIVES
IN A
SHELL

ISBN 978-0-545-61638-6

Text copyright © 2013 by Mike Thaler
Illustrations copyright © 2013 by Jared D. Lee Studio, Inc.

12 11 10 9 8 7 6 5 4   15 16 17 18/0

Printed in the U.S.A.   40
First printing, September 2013

BAD
BREATH

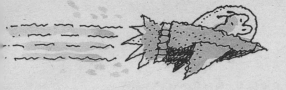

ROVER IN HIS ROCKET

CONTENTS

ZOMBIE PENGUIN

CHAPTER 1
KNOCK ON WOOD

Let's get one thing straight. I am not superstitious.

Cross my heart. But I *am* cautious.

LOCATION OF HEART

I never walk under a ladder or step on a crack. And I always carry my lucky rabbit's foot with me, even though it was not lucky for the rabbit.

I'M HAVING A BAD DAY.

If you are not superstitious, go ahead and finish reading my terrible tale. And good luck.

CHAPTER 2
A PARTY POOPER

I'm having a birthday next Friday. It happens every year. That's good. But Mom's giving me a birthday party. That's bad. It could be horrible.

 ⟵ TV PERSONALITY

9

What if no one comes? Or, what if everyone comes and no one brings a present? Or, everyone comes and brings a present I don't like.

Last year, everyone brought me gloves. I had sixteen pairs of gloves. I finally had to give them all away to the "Octopus Relief Fund."

Well, it's a week away. I'm not going to worry about it.

MOM, HERE'S THE PLACE I WAS TELLING YOU ABOUT.

THANK YOU!

LEAVE DONATIONS HERE

11

CHAPTER 3
GUESS WHO'S COMING?

THESE CARDS ARE GOOFY.

ARE THERE ANY CUTE PUPPY CARDS?

CORNY →

Mom is going to send out invitations to all my friends. The cards in the store are all corny. One has clowns, one has balloons, and one has kittens in party hats.

Forget it. I'll make my own. I'll

MOUSE WEARING A PARTY HAT →

draw a rainbow dinosaur blowing a horn. On the inside, I'll write, "Come to my party and bring a good present."

Mom says that's not polite.

"How about: *Please* come to my party and bring a good present?" I ask.

She shakes her head.

"Okay, then: There's going to be a party. Oh, boy!" I say.

Mom says that's too eager.

"Hey, if you're not doing anything next Friday, come to my party?"

Mom says that's too cool.

"What about: It's finally here. You've waited a whole year for it—my birthday party!"

Mom smiles. "That's good."

←— PIRANHA

I print them out, address the envelopes, put in the cards, and seal them up. Mom gives me stamps and asks if I put the time and date on the invitation.

Uh-oh. I can put that on the back of the envelope. September 13th at 5:00 p.m.

I take them down to the corner mailbox and drop them in.

STRING ⟶

NOT REAL ⟵

CHAPTER 4
PARTY ARTY

Now Mom says we have to get decorations. I think the house is fine already. It's decorated. I've got a monster poster on the wall and my model airplane hanging from the ceiling.

COOL.

SCARY.

RECLINER CHAIR ⟶

CONFETTI →

Mom drags me to the party store, anyway. Do you believe there's a whole store with *stuff* just for parties? They've got hats, balloons, banners, confetti, streamers, posters, signs, horns, and a thousand other useless *use me once and throw me away* things. Mom goes wild. She buys *everything*. Our house is going to look like Times Square on New Year's Eve. At least there are no flowers, no kittens, and nothing pink.

HAPPY BIRTHDAY

Then she says we have to get party favors for each kid. We have to give *them* presents?!!! It's *my* birthday. Now, if no one comes, I'll really feel bad. I'll have to wear all the party hats, and blow all the horns myself. Bummer. I'm glad this only happens once a year.

CHAPTER 5

GUEST GUESS

COYOTE ↓

On the school bus, I listen closely to hear if anyone got their invitations yet. No one says a word. I mailed them a day ago. What if they all got lost in the post office? I would have to play musical chairs by myself. At least I'd win.

Freddy says there's a circus in town. A circus! I can't compete with that! No way! I have an inflatable elephant, but they have a *real* one. I guess no one's going to come. I wonder if there's a market for never-used party hats?

I'll give a little hint to my friends on the bus.

"Hey, my birthday is coming up!" I shout.

Everyone just keeps on talking.
"Soon it will be my birthday!"
Everyone's quiet.
"I was born next Friday!" I yell.

Penny looks up.

"Are you going to start wearing diapers?" She giggles.

I shake my head.

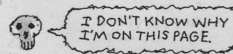

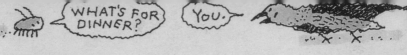

"Oh, are you having a party?" asks Doris.

"Sort of."

"Am I invited?" whines Doris.

"Maybe."

"Who else is coming?" sighs Doris.

"I don't know."

"Is it a circus party?" asks Freddy.

"No."

DORIS

FREDDY

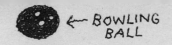 ← BOWLING BALL

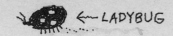 ← LADYBUG

"A movie party?" asks Eric.

"No."

"An ice-skating party?" asks Doris.

"No."

"A bowling party?" asks Derek.

"No."

"Well, what kind of party is it?" asks Randy.

ERIC   DEREK   RANDY

27

"A surprise party!" I answer.

"How can it be a surprise if you already know about it?" asks Penny.

"I'll be surprised if anyone comes."

28

WORM→ APPLE→

CHAPTER 6
THE APPLE CART

HELLO.

HUBIE, IT'S ERIC.

FROG

I'm feeling pretty bad.

Then Eric calls. "I got your card," he says.

"Good," I say.

"Your birthday is September 13th?" he asks.

"Every year," I answer.

"Your party is on *Friday*," he says, surprised.

"Next Friday," I answer.

"I can't come," he says.

"Why not?" I ask.

"I can't leave the house," he says.

"Are you grounded?"

PARTY ANIMAL

"No," he says.

"Well, why can't you come to my party?"

"Your party is on *Friday the 13th*!" he shouts.

There's a long silence.

"*Friday the 13th!!!*" he shouts again, and starts humming spooky music, then hangs up.

YELLING!!

CHAPTER 7
RSVP

"Mom, Eric's not coming to my party."

"Why?" she asks.

"Mom, this year my birthday falls on *Friday the 13th*."

"So?"

SOMETHING SMELLS FISHY.

"Mom, *Friday the 13th*. Don't you know that's the unluckiest, scariest day of the year?!"

"Oh, Hubie, that's just a silly superstition, and besides, it's too late to change it. We've already mailed out the invitations."

"Silly or not, my best friend is *not* coming, and I wonder who else won't show up."

HUBIE'S BEST FRIEND EVER →

WORRIED

INVITATION

CHAPTER 8
KING FOR A DAY

Mrs. Green heard that Friday is my birthday. I have to wear a silly crown all day long. How humiliating.

THREE CHEERS FOR THE BIRTHDAY BOY.

HOORAY! HOORAY! HOORAY!

PAPER CROWN

BRAVO!

36

QUEEN BEE ⟶

Mr. Bender will announce it over the loudspeaker. Everyone will know, but no one will come to my party. I wish I was never born.

GOOD MORNING, TEACHERS AND STUDENTS. I HAVE AN ANNOUNCEMENT TO MAKE.

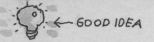

CHAPTER 9
GREAT IDEA!

HUMM....

After class, I tell Mrs. Green my problem.

"That's just a silly superstition," she says.

"Silly or not, everyone's afraid to come to my party," I say.

"A lot of the things that people are afraid of are just in their heads."

↑ TINY SNAKE

"Yeah, but it's *real* to them."

"Hey, Hubie, why not have a 'silly superstition' birthday party? Everyone could come as their favorite lucky charm."

"Will you come?" I ask.

"I wouldn't miss it for the world," says Mrs. Green.

CHAPTER 10

BORN TO BE GREAT

When I go to the library, Mrs. Beamster gives me a book called *The Birthday Book*. She says it's for the *birthday boy*. It's full of birthday stuff, like all the famous people born in September. There are lots of them.

There's kings, queens, and even emperors. There's generals and presidents. There's sport stars and movie stars, but best of all, there's a lot of great writers.

There's H. A. Rey, H. G. Wells,
T. S. Eliot, and Shel Silverstein.
That's great because *I* want to
be a writer. Mrs. Beamster says
I was born in a good month for
writers.

H.A. REY

H. G. WELLS

T. S. ELIOT

SHEL SILVERSTEIN

But maybe I'll have to add more initials to my name. I'll change it to M. T. Hubie.

CHAPTER 11
WAIT WEIGHT

It's here . . . Friday the 13th. All the decorations are up, all the candles are on the cake, and my room is relatively clean, so I just sit down and wait.

Maybe one of my presents will be a Ferrari. Maybe someone will bring me a new video game. I don't want any clothes, especially not gloves.

BRILLIANT SHINE ↘

FERRARI ↓

VERY EXPENSIVE ↓

HUGE ENGINE →

← EXTREMELY FAST

Well, it's 4:56. T-minus four minutes. I hope *someone* comes. If I have to eat the whole cake by myself, I'll get sick. Well, it's five o'clock . . . zero hour . . . blast off!

Now it's 5:01.

No one's here. I'm a failure. Mr. Unpopular. No one loves me. No one even likes me. They're all at the circus having fun. I don't care. Let them eat popcorn!

CHAPTER 12
PARTY ANIMAL

There's a knock at the door. I run to open it. It's Freddy! He's dressed like a giant rabbit's foot. I knew the cake would get him. He comes in and hands me a big box. It's light. I shake it. It rattles. It's not a Ferrari.

Then the doorbell rings again. It's Derek, Randy, Penny, Doris, and Eric.

Derek is dressed up as a horseshoe, Randy has his pants on backwards, Penny is a lucky penny, Doris is a ladybug, and Eric is a four-leaf clover. It's great to see them, and they *all* have presents.

Then Mrs. Green arrives. She's dressed as a rainbow and she's carrying a pot of gold that turns out to be chocolate candy kisses.*

RAINBOW HAT

RAINBOW TAIL

YUMMY

NEIGHBOR'S DOG

*Mr. Hershey was born on September 13th, too.

50

CHOCOLATE CANDY KISS

They hand me their presents. I weigh them and shake them. I guess it would be rude to open them now. I'll wait until they're all in the door. Mom takes all the presents and puts them on a table. Killjoy.

← NEIGHBOR'S BUG

She says, "Hubie, be a good host."

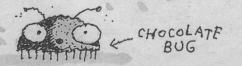

← CHOCOLATE BUG

CHAPTER 13
THE HOST WITH THE MOST

I say, "Won't you all please sit down?"

Everyone sits down and stares at me.

I say, "Simon says, 'Stand up.'"

Everyone stands up.

CAN WE REST NOW?

I say, "Simon says, 'Everyone open your presents.'"

Mom says, "Simon says, 'Be a good host.'"

"But, Mom, Simon wants to know what presents he got."

"*HUBIE!*" insists Mom.

"Okay, okay, Simon says, 'Forget it.'"

Instead, we play lots of games, like hide-and-seek. Freddy tries to hide in my closet and we have to dig him out. We also play Pin the Tail on the Donkey. Randy pins it on a lampshade; Eric pins it on Randy.

Then we play musical chairs. Eric and Penny are the only ones left. Penny loses because she tells Eric, "Ladies first"—but Eric just sits down.

I HATE THAT GAME.

54

Then Mom brings out hot dogs and potato salad. I don't really like coleslaw. I like macaroni salad a little, but I *love* potato salad. It's great to be the birthday boy.

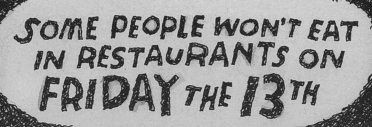

CHAPTER 14
MY LUCKY DAY

After we finish eating, Mom turns out the lights and brings in the cake with all the candles lit. Everyone sings "Happy Birthday." Then they all say, "Make a wish."

I close my eyes and think to myself, *I wish I could have a birthday every day.*

Then I take a big breath and blow.

TAKING A BIG BREATH →

HAPPY THOUGHTS.

58

"What did you wish for?" asks Doris.

"He can't tell or it won't come true," says Randy.

The cake is chocolate with chocolate frosting—my favorite. I eat the cake fast to get to the frosting. Then everyone opens their party favors and blows their horns, and they sing "Happy Birthday" to me again.

60

We all run around the table and fall down on the floor, laughing.

"Hey, open your presents," says Eric.

You know, I forgot all about the presents. We were having so much fun, I hated to stop.

I finally did open them and they were fine. I got the new video game I wanted, a cool pair of sunglasses, and lots of other stuff. But you know, I learned something on my birthday.

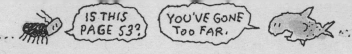

I learned that the best present is the *presence* of my friends, and the joy that they bring every day to my life.

63

This is my best birthday party ever, and I even blew out *all* of the candles. That means I'll have good luck for a year!